# SPECIAL OFFERS FOR MR MEN AND LITTLE MISS READERS

In every Mr Men and Little Mken.
Collect only six tokens and we w                                    choice
featuring all your favourit

And for the first 4,000 readers           ...om, we will send you a
Mr Men activity pad* and a bookmark* as well – absolutely free!

**Return this page with six tokens from Mr Men and/or Little Miss books to:**
Marketing Department, World International Limited, Deanway Technology Centre,
Wilmslow Road, Handforth, Cheshire SK9 3ET.

Your name:_____

Address:_____

_____

_____ Postcode: _____

Signature of parent or guardian: _____

I enclose **six** tokens – please send me a Mr Men poster  ☐

I enclose **six** tokens – please send me a Little Miss poster  ☐

We may occasionally wish to advise you of other children's books that
we publish. If you would rather we didn't, please tick this box  ☐

*while stocks last   *(Please note: this offer is limited to a maximum of two posters per household.)*

Collect six of these tokens.
You will find one inside every
Mr Men and Little Miss book
which has this special offer.

## 1 TOKEN

Please remove this page carefully

# Join the
## MR.MEN & little miss
## Club

Treat your child to membership of the long-awaited Mr Men & Little Miss Club and see their delight when they receive a personal letter from Mr Happy and Little Miss Giggles, a club badge **with their name on**, and a superb Welcome Pack. And imagine how thrilled they'll be to receive a card from the Mr Men and Little Misses on their birthday and at Christmas!

Take a look at all of the great things in the Welcome Pack, every one of them of superb quality (*see box right*). If it were

on sale in the shops, the Pack alone would cost around £12.00. But a year's membership, including all of the other Club benefits, costs just **£7.99** (plus 70p postage) with a 14 day money-back guarantee if you're not delighted.

To enrol your child please send **your** name, address and telephone number together with **your child's** full name, date of birth and address (including postcode) and a cheque or postal order for £8.69 (payable to Mr Men & Little Miss Club) to: Mr Happy, Happyland (Dept. WI), PO Box 142, Horsham RH13 5FJ. Or call 01403 242727 to pay by credit card.

**Please note:** We reserve the right to change the terms of this offer (including the contents of the Welcome Pack) at any time but we offer a 14 day no-quibble money-back guarantee. We do not sell directly to children - all communications (except the Welcome Pack) will be via parents/guardians. After 31/12/96 please call to check that the price is still valid. Please allow 28 days for delivery. Promoter: Robell Media Promotions Limited, registered in England number 2852153.

## The Welcome Pack:
✓ Membership card
✓ Personalized badge
✓ Club members' cassette with Mr Men stories and songs
✓ Copy of Mr Men magazine
✓ Mr Men sticker book
✓ Tiny Mr Men flock figure
✓ Personal Mr Men notebook
✓ Mr Men bendy pen
✓ Mr Men eraser
✓ Mr Men book mark
✓ Mr Men key ring

## Plus:
✓ Birthday card
✓ Christmas card
✓ Exclusive offers
✓ Easy way to order Mr Men & Little Miss merchandise

**All for just £7·99!** (plus 70p postage)

# MR. HAPPY

### by Roger Hargreaves

3 AUG 96

Coni – I grew up
loving these books,
and I think you're
the perfect person
to get "Mr. Happy"!
With love from
England –
Kim x

WORLD INTERNATIONAL

On the other side of the world, where the sun shines hotter than here, and where the trees are a hundred feet tall, there is a country called Happyland.

As you might very well expect everybody who lives in Happyland is as happy as the day is long. Wherever you go you see smiling faces all round. It's such a happy place that even the flowers seem to smile in Happyland.

And, as well as all the people being happy, all the animals in Happyland are happy as well.

If you've never seen a mouse smile, or a cat, or a dog, or even a worm — go to Happyland!

This is a story about someone who lived there who happened to be called Mr Happy.

Mr Happy was fat and round, and happy!

He lived in a small cottage beside a lake at the foot of a mountain and close to a wood in Happyland.

One day, while Mr Happy was out walking through the tall trees in those woods near his home, he came across something which was really rather extraordinary.

There in the trunk of one of the very tall trees was a door.

Not a very large door, but nevertheless a door. Certainly a door. A small, narrow, yellow door.

Definitely a door!

"I wonder who lives here?" thought Mr Happy to himself, and he turned the handle of that small, narrow, yellow door.

The door wasn't locked and it swung open quite easily.

Just inside the small, narrow, yellow door was a small, narrow, winding staircase, leading downwards.

Mr Happy squeezed his rather large body through the rather thin doorway and began to walk down the stairs.

The stairs went round and round and down and down and round and down and down and round.

Eventually, after a long time, Mr Happy reached the bottom of the staircase.

He looked around and saw, there in front of him, another small, narrow door. But this one was red.

Mr Happy knocked at the door.

"Who's there?" said a voice. A sad, squeaky sort of voice. "Who's there?"

Mr Happy pushed open the red door slowly, and there, sitting on a stool, was somebody who looked exactly like Mr Happy, except that he didn't look happy at all.

In fact he looked downright miserable.

"Hello," said Mr Happy. "I'm Mr Happy."

"Oh, are you indeed," sniffed the person who looked like Mr Happy but wasn't. "Well, my name is Mr Miserable, and I'm the most miserable person in the world."

"Why are you so miserable?" asked Mr Happy.

"Because I am," replied Mr Miserable.

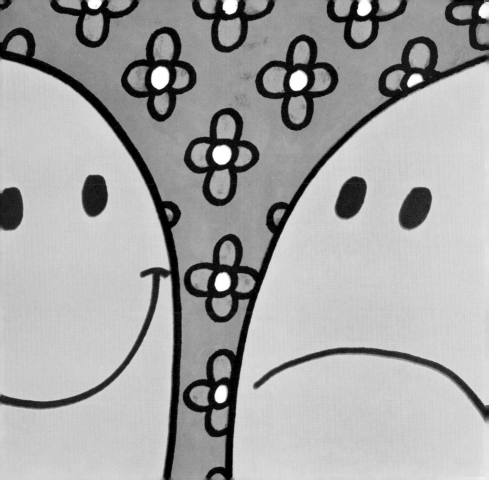

"How would you like to be happy like me?" asked Mr Happy.

"I'd give anything to be happy," said Mr Miserable. "But I'm so miserable I don't think I could ever be happy," he added miserably.

Mr Happy made up his mind quickly. "Follow me," he said.

"Where to?" asked Mr Miserable.

"Don't argue," said Mr Happy, and he went out through the small, narrow, red door.

Mr Miserable hesitated, and then followed.

Up and up the winding staircase they went. Up and up and round and round and up and round and round and up until they came out into the wood.

"Follow me," said Mr Happy again, and they both set off through the wood back to Mr Happy's cottage.

Mr Miserable stayed in Mr Happy's cottage for quite some time. And during that time the most remarkable thing happened.

Because he was living in Happyland Mr Miserable ever so slowly stopped being miserable and started to be happy.

His mouth stopped turning down at the corners.

And ever so slowly it started turning up at the corners.

And eventually Mr Miserable did something that he'd never done in the whole of his life.

He smiled!

And then he chuckled, which turned into a giggle, which became a laugh. A big booming hearty huge giant large enormous laugh.

And Mr Happy was so surprised that he started to laugh as well. And both of them laughed and laughed.

They laughed until their sides hurt and their eyes watered.

Mr Miserable and Mr Happy laughed and laughed and laughed and laughed.

They went outside and still they laughed.

And because they were laughing so much everybody who saw them started laughing as well. Even the birds in the trees started to laugh at the thought of somebody called Mr Miserable who just couldn't stop laughing.

And that's really the end of the story except to say that if you ever feel as miserable as Mr Miserable used to you know exactly what to do, don't you?

Just turn your mouth up at the corners.

Go on!